1.1/.5

 little bea

daniel roode

SCHOLASTIC INC.

New York Toronto London Auckland
Sydney Mexico City New Delhi Hong Kong

ISBN 978-0-545-45353-0

Copyright © 2011 by Daniel Roode.
All rights reserved. Published by Scholastic Inc., 557 Broadway, New York, NY 10012,
by arrangement with HarperCollins Children's Books, a division of HarperCollins Publishers.
SCHOLASTIC and associated logos are trademarks and/or registered trademarks of Scholastic Inc.

12 11 10 9 8 7 6 5 4 3 2 1   12 13 14 15 16 17/0

Printed in the U.S.A.   08

First Scholastic printing, January 2012

Adobe Illustrator and Adobe Photoshop were used to prepare the full-color art.
The text type is Martin Gothic URW T Light.

For Mom and Dad, and Laura

Up, up, up comes the sun.

A little bee spreads her wings and yawns.
"Good morning, Little Bea," says the sun.
"It's time to start the day!"

Bzzz. Bzzz. Bzzz!
Little Bea scoots from her flower and takes off.
Flutter. Flutter. Flutter. Hello, Butterfly!
Bzzz. Bzzz. Bzzz.
Little Bea buzzes as she flies by.

Knock, knock!

"Whoooooo's there?" says Owl.

"It's Bea."

"Bea who?"

"Be my friend and come play with me!"

Hoo-hoo-hooray!

Beaver is gathering pears, and Little Bea helps.
"Come back for pie tomorrow," says Beaver.
Bzzz. Bzzz. Bzzz. Yum!

Tug. Tug. Tuuuuug!
Little Bea helps Rabbit in his garden.
"One, two, carrots for you!"
Munch, munch, crunch.
"Thank you for lunch, Little Bea."

"Grrreetings, Little Bea," says Bear.
A flower for Bea.
Honey for Bear.
Bea and Bear love to share.

"Peekaboo! I see you!"

"I see you, too," says Deer.

Pitter. Patter. Drip. Drip. Drop.
Rain. Rain. Rain.
"I love the rain!" says Mouse.
"Let's play!" says Little Bea.
Bzzz! Bzzz! Splash!

"Chirp, chirp, chirp," says Cricket.
"Look, Little Bea, the sun is setting."

Bzzz. Bzzz. Bzzz.
Time to go home.

"Follow me!"
says Firefly.
Blink. Blink. Blink.

Up, up, up comes the moon.
Little Bea's friends are sleeping.
It's time for Little Bea to go to sleep, too.

"Hushhh . . . ," says the moon.

Good night, Little Bea.
Bzz. Bzz. Zzzzzzzzzzzzzz.